Jessica The Frog

Matthew Tallent

illustrated by Schenker De Leon

To order additional copies of this book, contact:
Xlibris
1-800-455-039
www.xlibris.com.au
Orders@Xlibris.com.au

Illustrated by Schenker De Leon

ISBN: Softcover   978-1-7960-0758-9
         Hardcover   978-1-7960-0759-6
         EBook   978-1-7960-0757-2

Print information available on the last page

Rev. date: 10/18/2019

Jessica The Frog

Matthew Tallent

When Jessica was born, she stunned everybody, including her parents. She had the rarest pink eyes that any of the other frogs had ever seen.

But her parents loved her just the same.

As she grew up, she struggled with her confidence as all the other frogs stared and pointed at her. Jessica felt like she didn't fit in.

She spent most of her time by herself beside the pond, crying.

When she would arrive home in tears, her mother would ask her what was wrong. Jessica explained that everyone stared and pointed at her because of her eyes.

Her mother explained that she was special and that one day, she would be beautiful. She said, "Always remember this, Jessica: good things come in a variety of packages."

As Jessica grew up, she struggled with the way the other frogs treated her. They made fun of her, calling her names and bullying her. She tried to stay strong and not show her feelings towards others. She didn't want to show her weakness.

So Jessica often let out her feelings when she was alone. She always felt comfortable and safe when she spent time alone in the garden.

As she spent more and more time in the garden, Jessica found that she was getting lonelier. Then day as she sat in the garden reading a book, a boy frog approached her.

"Hi, how is it going? My name is Peter. Wow, what beautiful eyes you have!"

Jessica answered, "Oh, yeah, you think?"

"Wwwhat?" Peter responded.

Jessica picked up her book and hopped off. Peter pursued her and said, "Hey, I was only trying to pay you a compliment."

Jessica replied, "Well, I don't need any compliments, thank you." And she walked off.

Peter was stunned.

The following day, she hopped back to her favourite garden. There was Peter, sitting there reading. She walked up to him and asked, "What are you doing here?"

"Reading," he replied.

"Well, why don't you find your own place to read."

"Hey, this is a free garden. Anyone can sit here." Jessica looked him, frustrated. Peter continued, "What's wrong? I'm only trying to be nice to you."

Jessica replied, "I'm sorry. Most of the frogs are always mean to me and call me names."

"Well, I won't," Peter assured her, "I'm not like all the other frogs."

Jessica and Peter sat there for ages, talking to each other. Peter told her he used to be called names as well. But when they did, he always responded, "Well, that's your opinion." And after a while, the frogs stopped bothering him. "In fact," Peter said, "we became friends. Hey, you can do the same! Or try it, if you like."

Jessica said, "I will."

Jessica and Peter talked for a long time and became friends. They agreed to meet up at the same time every day to discuss their likes and dislikes, as well as things they liked to do.

One day as Jessica was making her way to the garden, she passed some other frogs. As usual, they made comments about her appearance. And before she was about to say something back, she thought about what Peter had said. So she said, "Well, that's your opinion," and kept on hopping. The other frogs were stunned and didn't say anything more.

She meet up with Peter and discussed it with him. He said, "That's great!" So they sat there talking about general stuff.

Then Peter suddenly leant over and hugged Jessica. Jessica was surprised and blushed. Peter said, "I'm sorry."

Jessica said, "No, it's all right. I quite liked it." And they hugged again for the longest time.

After they stopped hugging. Peter looked at Jessica. He could tell that she was over the moon in love with him.

Shortly after that, one of Peter's friends, David, came up and asked them, "Hey, do you guys want to go to a party tonight?" Jessica and Peter decided to go home and change for the party.

Peter arrived early at the party near the pond. Everyone was having a great time doing bombs into the pond and chatting under a beautiful, moonlit sky, the light reflecting off the pond.

When Jessica arrived, everyone was gob smacked. Their mouths dropped, and conversations stopped. The sounds of the crickets and the water breaking were the only things that could be heard.

Jessica stood there, the most beautiful sparking glow came from her eyes. They looked like metallic pink paint. She had turned into one of the most stunning frogs in the land.

Peter walked up to her and said, "You're beautiful."

Jessica replied, "Thank you." And they finally kissed.

CPSIA information can be obtained
at www.ICGtesting.com
Printed in the USA
BVHW021415311019
562601BV00003B/14/P